A Doubleday Book for Young Readers
Published by
Random House Children's Books
a division of
Random House, Inc.
1540 Broadway, New York, New York 10036

Doubleday and the anchor with dolphin colophon
are registered trademarks of Random House, Inc.

Text by Thierry Robberecht
Illustrations by Philippe Goossens
Copyright © 2000 by Clavis Uitgeverij Amsterdam-Hasselt
First American Edition 2002
English translation copyright © 2002 by Random House, Inc.
Visit us on the Web! www.randomhouse.com/kids
Educators and librarians, for a variety of teaching tools, visit us at www.randomhouse.com/teachers

Cataloging-in-Publication Data is available from the Library of Congress.
ISBN: 0-385-74629-6 (trade)   0-385-90850-4 (lib. bdg.)

The text of this book is set in 28-point Zemke Handletter.

Book design by Trish P. Watts
Manufactured in Belgium
September 2002
10 9 8 7 6 5 4 3 2 1

THIERRY ROBBERECHT   ILLUSTRATED BY PHILIPPE GOOSSENS

Stolen Smile

A DOUBLEDAY BOOK FOR YOUNG READERS

Yesterday, in the schoolyard,
I lost my smile. And everyone
was looking at me.

"Are you angry?" all the kids
wanted to know.
"Did someone step on your toe?"
my best friend, Justine, asked.
"No," I said quickly, trying hard to
smile. But I couldn't.

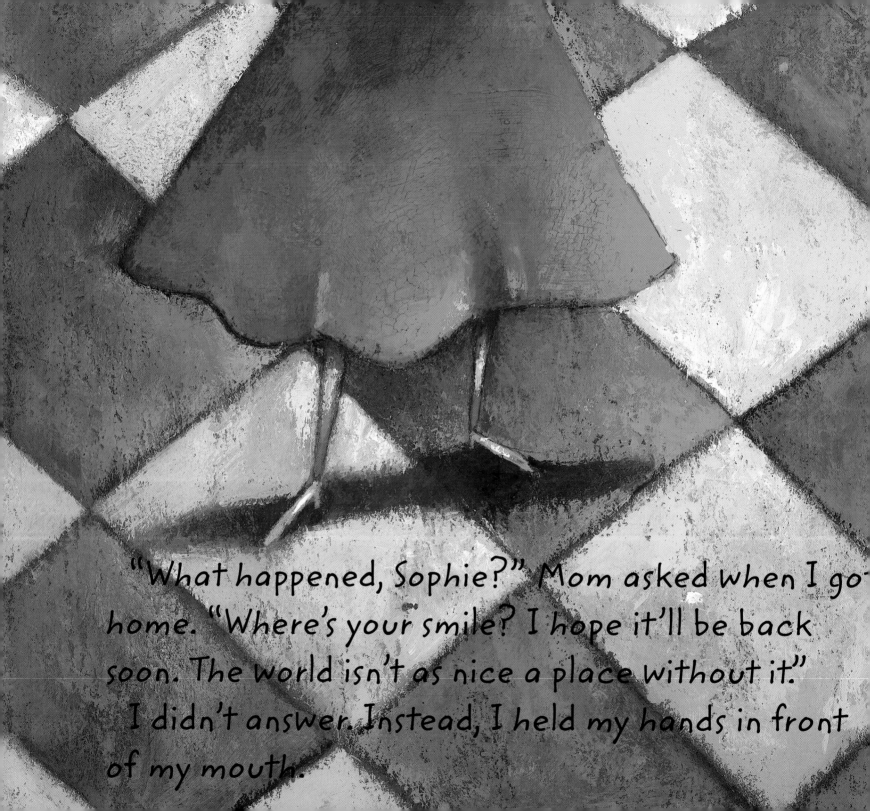

"What happened, Sophie?" Mom asked when I got home. "Where's your smile? I hope it'll be back soon. The world isn't as nice a place without it."

I didn't answer. Instead, I held my hands in front of my mouth.

"Just a minute," Daddy said later. "I know exactly how to make you smile." He left the room. When he returned, he was dressed up as a clown. He started making funny faces. Usually, Daddy is the funniest of all clowns, but I still did not smile. I told him I would rather sit on his lap.

Why did I always have to be smiling, anyway? I wondered. Did my mom and dad love me, or did they love my smile?

Besides, I knew where my smile was:
It was right on Willard's mouth. I'd
given him a smile and he had stolen it.

When I asked Willard to
play, he just started laughing.

Then Willard's friends laughed too. "We don't play with girls," they snickered.

My smile was spread all over their faces.

Aunt Grumbler stopped by that night and said it was my own fault.

"You shouldn't smile at just anyone," she grumbled. "Especially a silly boy. I bet Willard laughed because he likes you."

Mom told me not to worry, that I had plenty of smiles left. But I wasn't sure.

So this morning, I told Willard to give me back my smile.

"You're a silly boy," I said. "And I know something. You like me."

Willard's face turned cherry red. He didn't say a word. He didn't even laugh.

He was so surprised that he took a few steps backward and stumbled right over his book bag.

I helped him up. He smiled at me.

And that's when . . .

...I broke into a big smile too!